The Perfect
SWORD

SCOTT GOTO

ini Charlesbridge

SENSEI MASA was a master swordsmith known throughout all of Japan. His swords were considered some of the finest ever made. He and his apprentice, Michio, spent countless days and hours in the forge creating their swords. They heated and hammered the metal, over and over, to shape the blade. Then they polished and sharpened it to a razor's edge. Sensei and Michio took great care and effort and paid attention to every detail.

Once a sword was complete, both master and apprentice inspected it for flaws.

"Magnificent!" exclaimed Michio as he and Sensei studied their latest creation. "It is perfect."

"No," replied Sensei, his eyes still on the blade. "Nothing is truly perfect. Something can always be improved. Remember to try your very best in everything you do and continue to grow and learn."

"Yes, Sensei," replied Michio, with a slight bow.

"However," mused Sensei, "one could say my best is perfect."

Sensei turned to Michio and winked. Both burst into laughter.

"Now comes the hard part," sighed the master,
"finding an owner for this sword."

"But Sensei," replied the apprentice, "there are
hundreds of samurai in the city. Why should it be
difficult?"

"Many, yes," answered Sensei. "But not all are worthy.
Most are thugs and bullies who do not follow
Bushido. A sword is the soul of a samurai.
A just sword must have a just owner."

News of the sword spread fast. Soon a samurai came to buy it. Michio was sweeping the entrance floors one morning when suddenly he was lifted off his feet. A giant of a man held Michio high in the air with only one arm.

"Tell your master," the visitor bellowed while shaking the small apprentice, "that the great Katsuo is here to buy his sword!" He then dropped Michio back on his feet.

Michio stood shocked, staring at the ferocious-looking man. He then bowed with a "Yes, sir."

How strong and confident he is! thought Michio, running inside to find Sensei. *Someone like this must be a great warrior and worthy of our sword.*

"I have easily defeated hundreds of men!" roared Katsuo as he sat with Sensei. "I have captured countless villages! All who see me run in fear! Only one as strong as I deserves such a perfect sword!"

"And what if," asked Sensei, "the villagers don't want to work for you?"

"Hah!" snorted Katsuo. "Then I burn their houses and destroy all they own for questioning me!"

"I'm sorry," Sensei calmly replied, "but you are far too cruel and arrogant for this sword. Thank you for stopping by."

Katsuo was furious. He stormed out of the swordsmith's house, shouting curses at the master and the apprentice.

At first Michio was puzzled by Sensei's decision. However, after some thought he realized that a sword born of humility must go to one who is truly humble.

The next morning Michio was cleaning the screen doors when four men carrying a sedan chair stopped in front of him. They were surrounded by many servants and guards. Everyone in the party bowed deeply as an elegantly dressed man emerged from the chair.

"Announce to your master," shouted one of the servants, "that the noble Lord Toda is here to purchase the famous sword!"

Michio looked at Lord Toda, who had not once turned his way. He then bowed to the servant and went inside.

What power, to have so many people serving him, Michio thought. A man of such stature must be worthy of our sword.

"I have much political power and influence," explained Lord Toda to Sensei. "I have hundreds of servants and warriors who do my every bidding. Truly only one as noble as I deserves such a perfect sword."

"And how many battles have you fought in?" asked Sensei.

"Me, fight in battle? Never," replied Lord Toda. "I leave that to the soldiers. Such is the privilege of being born a noble."

"I'm sorry," replied Sensei. "You have earned nothing for yourself. This sword is not for you. Thank you for coming by."

Insulted and flustered, Lord Toda quickly left the swordsmith's house.

Again Michio was puzzled. But after much thought he realized that only one who has worked hard deserves a sword born of hard work.

The following day a tiny housefly was bothering Michio as he polished the entrance floors. Michio was swatting at it when a visitor appeared out of nowhere, startling him. The stranger had a stone-cold face, and yet his eyes burned like hot coals.

"Excuse me," the man whispered. "My name is Kenshin. I am a ronin. I wish to purchase the sword from your master."

"Yes, sir," said Michio as he tried to swat the fly that continued to annoy him. In an instant Kenshin drew his sword, sliced the fly in half, and placed his sword back in its scabbard.

Michio stood in awe of the expressionless ronin. He then bowed and went to find his master.

Surely Sensei will like this one, Michio thought. *Such calm and skill—he's the perfect candidate.*

"I have dedicated my life to Kenjutsu," said the ronin to Sensei. "All that matters to me is winning duels and perfecting my skill. Only one who is as dedicated as I should own such a perfect sword."

"And how do you think the shogun and lords treat the people?" asked Sensei.

."I have no interest in politics or such trivial matters," said Kenshin. "I only care about becoming the best swordsman in Japan."

"I'm sorry," replied Sensei. "You are dedicated, but you are also selfish. This sword is not for you. Thank you for coming by."

Kenshin bowed his head to the floor and left in silence.

Once more Michio was puzzled. Then he realized that a sword born of care and concern must go to one who cares for others, not just for himself.

Days passed and many more visitors came, but none was the right one. They were all either too cruel, too privileged, or too selfish.

Growing tired of meeting these people, Sensei and Michio took a day off to visit the marketplace. Nibbling on sticks of sweet candy, they walked by vendors who were selling everything from fish and vegetables to dishes and toys.

Both master and apprentice were enjoying the excitement of the
crowd when a large man shoved past them in a rush.

"Stop, thief!" cried out a vendor.

Before Sensei and Michio could do anything, a young man blocked
the thief's path. He was much smaller than the thief, but his body
looked strong and he had two swords, one long and one short,
stuck in his sash.

"Please return the money," the young samurai said to the thief.

"Out of my way, runt!" yelled the thief, and he pulled out
a large knife and slashed at the samurai.

The young warrior quickly disarmed the thief and knocked him unconscious. His hand never once reached for either of his swords.

Michio was amazed. Sensei nodded in approval.

"Thank you for your help," the vendor said to the samurai. "Please, take these coins as a reward."

"One should not be rewarded for doing what is right," replied the samurai. "Thank you, but no."

As the young samurai walked away, Sensei turned to Michio and said, "Go and invite him to our house. Tell him who we are, but do not say why we wish to meet him."

Michio nodded and ran after the young man. Sensei headed home to prepare for his guest.

Not long after, the samurai sat with Sensei in his house as Michio served
hot tea.

"My name is Takeshi," said the young man, bowing low. "I am a low-ranking
samurai in my clan. It is an honor to be here, Sensei Masa. Your work is
respected throughout Japan."

"It is I who am honored to meet you," replied Sensei, with a bow.
"But tell me, why did you not draw your sword today while fighting that thief?"

an act of weakness, not strength. I would have dishonored my sword by drawing it today, and to dishonor the sword is to dishonor the soul."

Michio sat quietly on the side, listening with a smile.

"You are obviously very skilled," said Sensei.

"Not skilled enough," replied Takeshi. "Learning martial arts is never-ending and requires hard work; thus I train daily."

"And why," continued Sensei, "did you help today? Surely you did not know the vendor."

"I had the power to help," said Takeshi. "When one can, one should. Such is the responsibility of power, even with as little as I have."

"Excellent," replied Sensei. "You are the one we have been searching for."

Michio handed their latest creation to Sensei, who then gave it to Takeshi. The young samurai was speechless as he gazed at the sword. Michio sat down, fully understanding his master's decision.

"Let this sword," said the master, "help you grow as a warrior and as a person—in mind, body, and spirit."

Takeshi grasped the sword with both hands. "I will strive to be worthy of this most precious gift," he said, bowing his head to the floor.

Sensei and Michio then bid Takeshi farewell and watched him leave.

"Come, Michio," said the master.

"Is it time to start working on the next perfect soul, Sensei?" asked the apprentice.

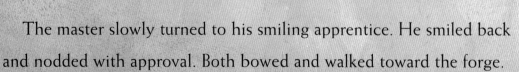

The master slowly turned to his smiling apprentice. He smiled back and nodded with approval. Both bowed and walked toward the forge.

SWORD MAKING IN ANCIENT JAPAN

The sword has had a long and varied history in Japanese culture, from the second century BC to modern times. I set this story at the beginning of the Tokugawa shogunate in the late 1500s. The shoguns ruled Japan for over 650 years, and their will was enforced by the samurai, or warrior, class.

Creating a samurai sword was a sacred art. The sword was considered the soul of the samurai, representing his honor and character. A Japanese swordsmith would often meditate, fast, or pray to cleanse his mind and soul before creating a samurai's sword.

Only the samurai were allowed to carry a pair of swords, one long and one short, called *daisho* (DIE-SHOH). The long sword, or *daito* (DIE-TOH), measured more than two feet in length. The short sword, called the *shoto* (SHOH-TOH) or *wakizashi* (wa-kee-ZA-shee), measured between one and two feet in length.

Although they do not appear in this story, many different craftsmen were involved in creating a Japanese sword. Swordsmiths created the main body, polishers sharpened the blade, wood-carvers made the scabbard, and other craftsmen created the finishings, such as the sword guard.

The Japanese master/apprentice relationship is very different from the Western model. Very rarely, if ever, does the apprentice ask questions. The apprentice usually stands back and observes the master. That is why Michio is left to come to his own conclusions as to why the swordsmen do not meet with Sensei's approval. In this story I wanted to stay true to the traditional roles that the apprentice and master would play in ancient Japan.

WORDS TO KNOW

Bushido (BOO-shee-doh): The samurai code of honor.

Kenjutsu (ken-joo-TSOO): The Japanese martial art of using a sword in combat.

ronin (ROH-nin): A samurai who has lost his master either by ruin or by falling out of favor.

samurai (SAH-muh-rye): A Japanese warrior who serves a daimyo, or lord.

sensei (SEN-say): A master or teacher.

shogun (SHOH-gun): A title meaning "general" that was given to the rulers of Japan from 1185 to 1868.

This book is dedicated to my sensei of lessons on life, my father: Victor Michio Goto

While creating this book my biggest concern was making sure it *felt* Japanese. I tried to convey this feeling through the way the characters are drawn—not by using a traditional Japanese style of art, but by focusing on the characters' mannerisms and facial expressions. For the text I tried to recreate the rhythm of the Japanese language in English. These mannerisms, expressions, and rhythms are based on the samurai movies I watched as a kid and, especially, on the family members I grew up with!

I hope readers will also notice and explore the more subtle elements of the story. Symbolism is a part of Japanese culture; many animals and plants represent human qualities and stations in life. I chose certain background imagery and Japanese names for their symbolic meanings. But most importantly, I hope the combination of all these elements makes the book a bit more fun to read!

Published by Charlesbridge
85 Main Street
Watertown, MA 02472
(617) 926-0329
www.charlesbridge.com

Library of Congress Cataloging-in-Publication Data
Goto, Scott.
The perfect sword / Scott Goto.
p. cm.
Summary: After a Japanese master swordmaker and his apprentice craft the
perfect sword, they search high and low for someone worthy of it.
ISBN 978-1-57091-697-7 (reinforced for library use)
[1. Swords—Fiction. 2. Samurai—Fiction. 3. Conduct of life—Fiction.
4. Japan—History—1185–1868—Fiction.] I. Title.
PZ7.G6937Pe 2008
[Fic]—dc22   2007017184

Printed in China
(hc) 10 9 8 7 6 5 4 3 2 1

Illustrations done in oil paints on paper
Display type set in Ryan, designed by Holly Goldsmith for Bitstream
Text type set in Weiss
Color separations by Chroma Graphics, Singapore
Printed and bound by Jade Productions
Production supervision by Brian G. Walker
Designed by Susan Mallory Sherman